# THE BUS FOR US
## NUESTRO AUTOBÚS

Suzanne Bloom

Translated by Aída E. Marcuse

BOYDS MILLS PRESS

AN IMPRINT OF HIGHLIGHTS

*Honesdale, Pennsylvania*

Text and illustrations copyright © 2001 by Suzanne Bloom
Spanish translation copyright © 2008 by Boyds Mills Press
All rights reserved
For information about permission to reproduce selections from this book,
please contact permissions@highlights.com.

Boyds Mills Press, Inc.
An Imprint of Highlights
815 Church Street
Honesdale, Pennsylvania 18431
Printed in China

The Library of Congress has cataloged the English hardcover edition as follows:

Bloom, Suzanne.
The bus for us / written and illustrated by Suzanne Bloom.—1st ed.
[32]p.: col. ill. ; cm.
Summary: On her first day of school, Tess wonders what the school bus will look like.
ISBN: 978-1-56397-932-3 (hc) • ISBN: 978-1-59078-629-1 (bilingual Spanish-English pb)
1. School — Fiction. 2. School buses — Fiction. I. Title.
[E]      21      2001      AC      CIP
00-102348
Bilingual (English-Spanish) Paperback ISBN: 978-1-62091-443-4

First bilingual (Spanish-English) edition, 2008
The text of this book is set in Palatino.

10 9 8 7 6 5 4 3 2 1

To four fabulous first-grade teachers and to Alice, who always asked
—SB

# Is this the bus for us, Gus?

¿Es éste nuestro autobús, Gus?

No, Tess. This is a taxi.

No, Tess. Éste es un taxi.

Is this the bus for us, Gus?

¿Es éste nuestro autobús, Gus?

No, Tess. This is a tow truck.

No, Tess. Ésta es una grúa.

BUS
STOP

# Is this the bus for us, Gus?

## ¿Es éste nuestro autobús, Gus?

No, Tess. This is a fire engine.

No, Tess. Éste es un camión de bomberos.

Is this the bus for us, Gus?

¿Es éste nuestro autobús, Gus?

No, Tess. This is an ice-cream truck.

No. Tess. Éste es un camión de helados.

Is this the bus for us, Gus?

¿Es éste nuestro autobús, Gus?

No, Tess. This is a garbage truck.

No, Tess. Éste es un camión de la basura.

# Is this the bus for us, Gus?
## ¿Es éste nuestro autobús, Gus?

No, Tess. This is a backhoe.

No, Tess. Ésta es una excavadora.

Is this the bus for us, Gus?

¿Es éste nuestro autobús, Gus?

Yes, Tess. This is the bus for us. Let's go!

Sí, Tess. Éste es nuestro autobús. ¡Vamos!

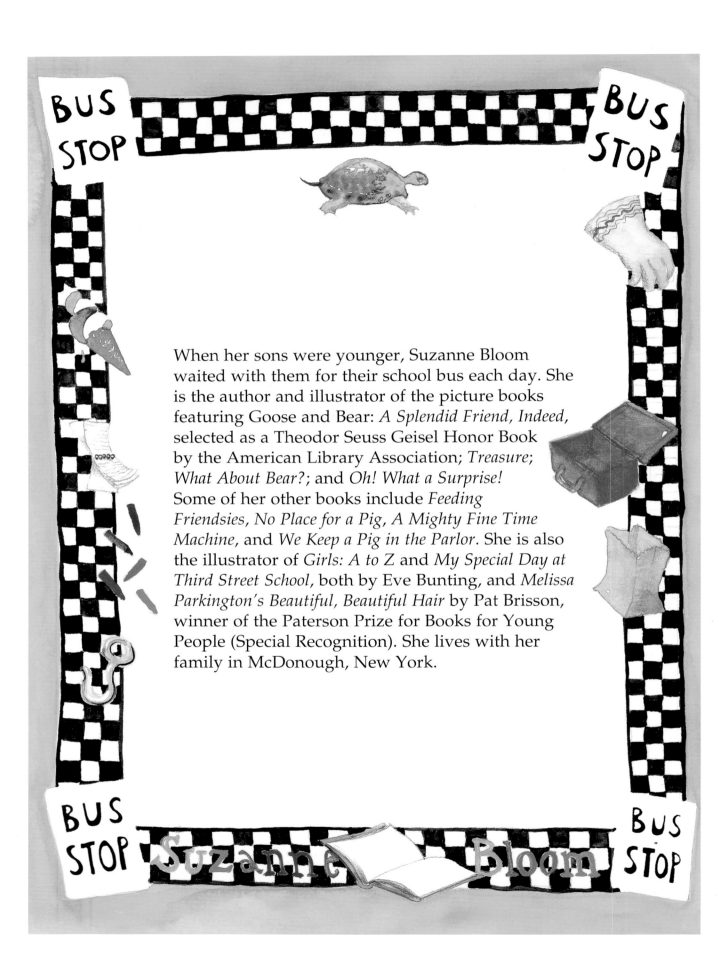

When her sons were younger, Suzanne Bloom waited with them for their school bus each day. She is the author and illustrator of the picture books featuring Goose and Bear: *A Splendid Friend, Indeed*, selected as a Theodor Seuss Geisel Honor Book by the American Library Association; *Treasure*; *What About Bear?*; and *Oh! What a Surprise!* Some of her other books include *Feeding Friendsies*, *No Place for a Pig*, *A Mighty Fine Time Machine*, and *We Keep a Pig in the Parlor*. She is also the illustrator of *Girls: A to Z* and *My Special Day at Third Street School*, both by Eve Bunting, and *Melissa Parkington's Beautiful, Beautiful Hair* by Pat Brisson, winner of the Paterson Prize for Books for Young People (Special Recognition). She lives with her family in McDonough, New York.